The Adventures of
BOB and RED

written and illustrated by
DAVID BARRON

LANDMARK EDITIONS, INC.

P.O. Box 270169 • 1402 Kansas Avenue • Kansas City, Missouri 64127
(816) 241-4919

Dedicated to:
My parents, who believe in me and
always encourage me to do my best.

With special thanks to Gary Judson,
the owner of the real "Bob", and to
Curtis Holborn, my favorite motorcyclist.

COPYRIGHT © 1999 BY DAVID BARRON

International Standard Book Number: 0-933849-71-0 (LIB.BDG.)

Library of Congress Cataloging-in-Publication Data
Barron, David 1988-
    The adventures of Bob and Red / written and illustrated by David Barron.
    p. cm.
    Summary: An old truck and an old tractor set out on an adventurous
trip to reach an antique car museum and save themselves from becoming
junked for scrap metal.
    ISBN 0-933849-71-0 (lib.bdg. : alk. paper)
    [1. Trucks—Fiction.   2. Tractors—Fiction.
    3. Friendship—Fiction.]

I. Title.
PZ7.B27563Ad   1999
[E]—dc21
                                          99-13494
                                          CIP

Creative Coordinator: David Melton
Editorial Coordinator: Nancy R. Thatch
Computer Graphics Coordinator: Brian Hubbard

Printed in the United States of America

Landmark Editions, Inc.
P.O. Box 270169
1402 Kansas Avenue
Kansas City, Missouri 64127
(816) 241-4919

Visit our Website — www.LandmarkEditions.com

THE ADVENTURES OF BOB AND RED

Through the years, some of the brothers and sisters of the winners of our NATIONAL WRITTEN & ILLUSTRATED...CONTEST have created books and entered them. A number of their books have competed very well, some making it into the top ten in an age category, and others advancing to the top five books.

I knew that someday one of their books would win. To tell the truth, I didn't look forward to that happening. I felt, if a book by a brother or sister won, people might wonder if our judges had shown it special favors. Nothing could be further from truth. I know that each and every book entered in the contest is judged strictly on the merits of the book itself and not according to the person who wrote and illustrated it.

In 1997 we received a book that was created by a seven-year-old boy named David Barron, who happened to be the brother of Kathryn Barron, the author/illustrator of CRITTER CRACKERS, a 1994 Publisher's Choice Gold Award Winner. David's book was a very good one, and it placed in the top five in the younger age category. In fact, it won Second Place.

But David is a very determined boy. In 1998 he created an even better book, THE ADVENTURES OF BOB AND RED, which won First Place! David's book did not win because Kathryn Barron is his sister. His book won because it was an excellent book, which is exactly the reason it should have won.

Now then, let me tell you some things about David. He is a very good writer. He is clever, and he knows how to write an exciting, funny, and often very touching story.

Moreover, David is an illustrator of the first caliber. I am accustomed to working with kids who have exceptional talents and skills, but when it comes to drawing and painting, this boy holds a handful of aces. He can really draw! He has the ability to visualize an object, such as a person, a ball, a rock, a tree, or a truck, and then he can mentally walk all the way around that object and draw it from any angle or perspective. Now, that's good for an adult artist, but for a nine-year-old, it's astounding!

David can really paint, too! He does not know that watercolors are supposed to be difficult to use, so he just brushes paint across the paper as easily as if he were roller-skating down a hill.

Adding to all of David's attributes as a writer and an illustrator, David is a very nice boy with whom to work. He is friendly, polite, eager, and alert, and an absolute pleasure.

David's book is a pleasure, too. It has the magic of a good story, and his amazing illustrations illuminate and extend every scene. On the surface, his exciting story tells readers about the last trip made by an old truck and an old tractor. But underneath, it becomes more than that. It becomes the story of two old friends who really care about the well-being of each other.

I think this book has everything. Besides having an exciting story and wonderful illustrations, it has "heart." I like that!

THE ADVENTURES OF BOB AND RED is a book to enjoy and admire. Just turn the pages and you'll see what I mean.

— David Melton
Creative Coordinator
Landmark Editions, Inc.

In the junkyard behind Dave's Garage, there were lots of old cars and trucks. Some had been in wrecks. They were damaged so badly, they couldn't be fixed. Others had been traded in by their owners.

Bob the Truck and Red the Tractor were two of these trade-ins. Farmer Jones had left them when he bought a new truck and tractor.

Bob and Red had been put up for sale, but no one had ever offered to buy them. So for several years, the two of them had stood in the junkyard, gathering rust and cobwebs.

One afternoon Bob the Truck let out a moan and opened his eyes.

"Are you okay?" asked Red the Tractor.

"I think so," groaned Bob. "But everything looks blurry. How long was I asleep?"

"About two years," Red answered.

"That was a long time!" exclaimed Bob.

"It sure was," replied Red. "But you're awake now because Dave gave you a new battery and put some gas in your tank. He gave me a

4

new battery, too, and he kicked my tires."

"I just hate it when anyone kicks my tires," Bob said.

"Yeah, me too," Red agreed.

"Anyway," Bob smiled, "I'm glad to be back with you, Red."

"Well, I'm not so red anymore," the old tractor grumbled. "Most of my paint has faded."

"I don't look so great either," said Bob. "My fenders are dented. But maybe Dave is planning to fix us up so he can sell us."

"No, he's not going to do that," said Red. "Dave told the man at the scrap metal plant to come and get us tomorrow."

"Oh, no!" exclaimed Bob. "If he takes us to that plant, we will be ground up into little pieces!"

"I know," Red sighed. "It looks like this is the end for us, old friend."

"It sure does," Bob replied sadly.

When it grew dark, Red went to sleep.

But Bob the Truck was so worried, he couldn't fall asleep.

About midnight Bob called out, "Hey, Red, wake up!"

Red opened his sleepy eyes and yawned.

"Was I snoring too loud?" he asked.

"Like a steam engine," Bob told him. "But that's not why I woke you. I wanted to ask you if you remembered that guy who owns the antique automotive museum in Birchville."

"You mean the man who came here three years ago — the one who was looking for old cars?" asked Red.

"That's the one," Bob said. "I'll bet if we could get to Birchville, he would fix us up and put us in his museum."

"But Birchville is more than a hundred miles from here," Red replied. "How could we get there?"

"We have new batteries," Bob reminded him, "and both of us have gas in our tanks."

"Well, I might have enough gas," said Red, "but you don't. Dave put only a gallon in your tank."

"That won't be a problem for me," Bob told him. "I can get some more gas on the way."

"How can you do that? You don't have any money."

"Yes, I do," Bob smiled proudly. "I've got a twenty-dollar bill in my glove compartment. Farmer Jones always kept a twenty there in case of an emergency. When he traded me in, he forgot to take the twenty dollars with him."

"Even if you have the money," said Red, "I don't think it would be a good idea for us to leave here."

Bob leaned forward and gave Red a serious look.

"If we don't go now," he warned, "we will be ground-up scrap metal by tomorrow night."

Red didn't have to think about that for very long. "Okay," he agreed. "Let's get out of here!"

Bob the Truck and Red the Tractor started their motors. Then they drove out of Dave's junkyard as quietly as they could.

Bob and Red rolled down the highway for about an hour.

Then Bob called to Red, "Old Bill's Gas Station should be just a couple of miles up the road."

They were glad to see the station was still there, but it looked a lot older. Its pumps were rusty and paint was peeling off the building. The office downstairs was dark, and a CLOSED sign hung on the door. But there was a light on in the apartment over the garage.

Red hid in the shadows at the side of the building. Bob pulled up to a pump and honked his horn several times.

Old Bill opened the upstairs window and yelled down, "Can't you see, I'm closed for the night?"

"But this is an emergency," replied Bob. "I'm out of gas!"

"Okay, okay!" Old Bill hollered back. He slammed the window shut and went downstairs. Then he turned on the light and hobbled outside in his pajamas and bathrobe.

"Give me twenty dollars worth," Bob told him.

Old Bill took the hose from the pump and poured gas into Bob's tank. But when he looked in the truck window, he didn't see a driver.

"Hey!" Old Bill called out, "Where are you?"

"I'm checking the tailgate," he heard a voice answer. "There's a twenty-dollar bill in the glove compartment. Just reach in and get it."

Old Bill did as he was told. Under an old newspaper, he found the twenty. He clutched the money tightly in his fist. Then he walked to the back of the truck to see if the driver needed any help.

"Hey, where did you go now?" he asked, looking around.

All he heard was the driver's door slam shut and the motor start. Then someone called out, "Thanks a lot!" and the truck drove away.

Old Bill just stood there for a few moments with a puzzled look on his face. Finally, he shrugged his shoulders, went back inside, and closed the door.

Red waited until Old Bill had turned out the light. Then he started his motor and pulled onto the highway to catch up with Bob.

Bob and Red headed north toward Birchville. At sunrise Bob flashed his right-turn signal light. They both pulled over to the side of the highway.

"I need to rest for a few minutes," Bob said, trying to catch his breath.

"I'm tired myself," Red told him. "I'm not as spry as I used to be."

Across the highway there was a large field of corn. Beyond that, a big red barn and a house stood at the top of a hill.

"Look at that farm," said Bob with a sigh. "It reminds me of the days when we worked for Farmer Jones."

"Yeah," replied Red. "We sure worked hard for him. I never thought he would leave us in a junkyard."

"That's the thanks we got for doing all that work," Bob said.

Suddenly they heard the roar of engines. A cloud of dust swirled up on the road and came straight toward them. Then two tough-looking men, named Big Bart and Bull, came into view on motorcycles.

Bob and Red began to tremble, but they didn't make a sound. They

hoped the riders would pass on by. To their horror, both motorcycles skidded to a stop right beside them.

"Well, look what someone left here, just for us," chuckled Big Bart.

Big Bart was the meanest-looking man Bob and Red had ever seen. They began to tremble even more when Big Bart said, "I wonder if there's anything inside that truck that we could use."

"Let's look and see," said the short, stocky man called Bull.

The two ruffians got off their motorcycles and swaggered over to the truck. Big Bart opened the door and climbed onto the driver's seat. He reached over and opened the glove compartment.

"There ain't nothin' here but an old newspaper," he grumbled.

"Them floor mats might be worth somethin'," said Bull as he climbed into the truck.

"I already seen those!" growled Big Bart. "I ain't stupid, you know!"

Big Bart reached down to yank up the floor mats.

And that's when it happened...

Without warning, both of Bob's doors slammed shut!

"What's going on?" Big Bart exclaimed.

"Let's get out of here!" hollered Bull.

They reached for the door handles. But before they could turn them, the locks on both doors snapped down — *Click! Click!*

"Hey, let us out!" they yelled.

Bob the Truck's motor started with a growl. His gas pedal hit the floorboard. His tires screeched into action. In an instant, the truck's speed went from zero to 60 miles per hour!

"We're trapped!" howled Big Bart as the truck zoomed down the highway. He and Bull yelled and screamed, and they pounded their fists on the windows!

Bob just laughed, and then he went even faster — 65 — 70 — 75 — 80 miles an hour!

Now Big Bart was really terrified! He stomped his foot on the brake pedal. The brakes didn't work! He tried to down-shift the gears. The

gear shift wouldn't budge! He grabbed hold of the key and pulled it out of the ignition. But the motor wouldn't turn off!

"Help!" yelled Big Bart. "We're gonna be killed!"

Now Bob went even faster — 85 miles an hour!

"I'm too young to die!" screamed Bull.

Soon Bob was going 90 miles an hour! Suddenly he swerved off the highway and headed straight for a huge oak tree. Big Bart tried to turn the steering wheel, but it was locked tight.

Big Bart yelled and hollered! Bull put his hands over his eyes and started to scream!

Bob pushed down his brake pedal. Just before he hit the tree, the truck screeched to a stop!

Suddenly, both doors unlocked — *Click! Click!*

And the doors sprang open — *Whop! Whop!*

Big Bart and Bull leaped out of the truck. They ran over the hill, yelling and screaming all the way.

Bob was still laughing as he pulled onto the highway and turned around. He drove back to where Red was waiting for him.

"Are you all right?" asked Red.

"Couldn't be better," Bob laughed. "I gave those guys the ride of their lives. I'll bet they haven't stopped running yet."

"They probably haven't," said Red, "but they won't stay away very long. They'll come back to get their motorcycles. And when they do, we don't want to be here."

"You're right," agreed Bob, "so we had better drive on."

"I can't drive in the daylight!" exclaimed Red. "Someone will notice that I don't have a driver."

"Well, we will just have to find a driver for you," replied Bob. He began looking around, trying to think of what to do. When he saw a scarecrow in the cornfield, he got an idea.

"Hey, you crows!" Bob called out to the birds who were perched on the telephone lines. "Could we talk to you for a minute?"

"Sure," squawked one of the crows, and he flew down and sat on the hood of the truck.

"What do you want?" asked the crow.

"Are you guys *really* scared of that scarecrow?" asked Bob.

"Are you kidding?" laughed the crow. "We don't pay any attention to that old bag of rags. We just let him stand there with that silly smile on his face."

"Well," said Bob, "my friend, Red the Tractor, needs a driver. I was wondering if we could borrow that scarecrow."

"That old thing?" laughed the crow. "You don't have to borrow him. You can take him and keep him!"

"That's wonderful!" exclaimed Bob.

"Hey, fellas," the crow called up to the others. "Come down here and give me some help. We're going to turn our old scarecrow into a super-duper driver!" he chuckled.

And that's exactly what the crows did.

The crows found a piece of rope. Then they tied the scarecrow to the tractor seat. Now Red had his driver.

"Thanks, guys," said Red, but he was worried. He looked back at the scarecrow that kept smiling at him. "Well," he said, "I sure hope this is going to work."

"It will," replied Bob as he started his motor. "It has to work."

Red started his motor, too, and he followed Bob onto the highway.

With each bump Red hit, the scarecrow bounced up and down and wobbled back and forth. But the rope held tight, and the scarecrow stayed on. And with that painted smile on his face, he looked as if he was even enjoying the trip.

"Now remember," Bob called to Red, "when we get to Plainfield, we don't want to call any attention to ourselves."

"That's right," Red agreed.

"So here's what we'll do," explained Bob. "When we drive into town, we must be sure not to go too fast, and we must not go too slow.

And we must be careful to stop at every stoplight."

"I'll remember," Red promised.

When they entered the town, Bob and Red were really nervous. They drove very carefully as they passed by the cafe, the hotel, and the *Shop 'N' Go* store.

There were many people in town. They were strolling up and down the sidewalks, crossing the streets, and looking in store windows. But no one seemed to notice the old truck or the smiling scarecrow that was tied on the old tractor. When Bob and Red saw their plan was working, they finally relaxed.

"Just stay calm," Bob whispered. "We'll soon be out of town."

Then, at the corner of Main and First streets, the stoplight turned from green to red. Bob and Red were paying close attention, so both of them pulled to a stop. Then they waited patiently for the light to change back to green.

But before the light had time to change...

Bang! Bang!

The sound of gunshots suddenly shattered the silence!

The doors of the bank burst open! A man and a woman, carrying guns and large sacks full of money, dashed outside.

Bang! Bang!

Their guns went off again.

As the robbers ran toward their car, something shiny slipped out of the woman's hand. It fell to the sidewalk and dropped through the grate by the curb.

"Charlie!" she screamed. "I've dropped our car keys!"

"Forget the keys, Sal!" Charlie yelled back. "We'll take that old truck that's over there!"

The truck the robbers ran to was none other than Bob!

Sal quickly leaped into the back of the truck.

Charlie jumped onto Bob's running board. He hit his gun against the door and yelled into the window, "Step on it, Buster!"

Bob was so frightened, he did exactly what the robber told him to do. He floor-boarded his gas pedal and ran the red light. He sped down Main Street, leaving two smoking streaks of black rubber on the pavement behind him.

When he reached the highway, Bob looked in his rearview mirror. Red was still following him, trying to keep up. The scarecrow was bouncing up and down and wobbling back and forth even more now. But he was still smiling his painted smile.

Then the shrill sound of a siren pierced the air.

When Bob looked back, he saw a police car with flashing lights on it. The police car passed Red and pulled in front of him.

"Oh, no!" cried Bob. "Now the police are after me! I'll be arrested and sent back to the junkyard!"

And the old truck tried to go even faster.

"Hurry up!" yelled Charlie, hitting his gun against the door. "The police are gaining on us!"

"Can't this piece of junk go any faster?" the woman yelled.

Piece of junk, indeed! Bob thought, and he pushed his gas pedal to the floor. The needle on the speedometer rose past 85 miles an hour. But the police car went even faster and kept getting closer and closer to the old truck.

When Charlie and Sal started shooting their guns, the police fired back. Bullets whizzed by to the left and to the right of Bob. And then one hit him in his left-rear fender.

"Ow!" Bob hollered. "I've been shot!"

"Hold on, Bob!" yelled Red. "I'm coming to help you!"

Red left the highway and crossed an open field. He got to the other side, just in time to pull in front of the police car.

"Get out of our way!" the policemen yelled at him.

Red got so excited that he spun around a curve on two wheels and skidded off the road. The rope that held the scarecrow on the seat broke, and the scarecrow was thrown high into the air. When he came

down, he landed on top of the windshield of the police car — *Splat!*

With the scarecrow spread out across their windshield, the police couldn't see to drive. Their car swerved off the highway and smashed into a fence, throwing the scarecrow into the middle of a field.

"Did you see the face on that guy?" one policeman asked.

"Yeah, it was really awesome!" the other exclaimed.

The policemen jumped out of their car and ran into the field. They tried to find the man who had been thrown from the tractor. But all they found was a lot of straw on the ground, an old hat, a plaid shirt, and a ragged pair of jeans.

"Looks like he's gone," said one policeman, "and he's left all his clothes behind."

"Well," the other policeman chuckled, "he's going to get pretty cold, running through the woods without any clothes on."

They both laughed, then hurried back to their police car. They got inside and headed down the highway to catch the robbers.

As Bob sped down the highway, the robbers held on tight.

"The cops stopped back there!" yelled Sal. "Let's jump off and let them chase this old truck for a while."

"Good idea!" Charlie yelled back. He hit his gun against Bob's door and ordered, "Stop this truck!"

Bob came to a screeching halt. The two robbers jumped off and pointed their guns at Bob.

"Now get goin' and don't look back!" yelled Charlie.

Bob was so scared, he drove away as fast as he could. But he did look back because he was so worried about Red. He couldn't see Red anywhere. All he saw were the flashing lights of the police car.

"They're after me again!" Bob cried out, and he tried to go faster.

Soon he heard the sound of thunder. There was a flash of lightning, and rain started to hit his windshield. He turned on his wipers, but the old blades didn't work very well. Bob could hardly see the road in front of him, and he panicked!

"What can I do?" he exclaimed. "I've got to find a place to hide!"

A stone bridge came into view ahead of him. Just before he reached it, he steered off the highway and drove down the slope into a small stream. He pulled under the bridge, turned off his lights and motor, and sat there trembling with fear.

Bob soon heard the police car approaching with its siren blaring. When the car stopped on the bridge, Bob sat very still and held his breath. The policeman's flashlight shone brightly as its beam swept back and forth across the ground.

"Can you see them?" Bob heard the driver ask.

"No, they're not here," the other policeman answered.

Then the siren wailed again, and the police car sped away.

Bob knew he had better stay hidden under the bridge. The water came up above his hubcaps. It was freezing! Poor Bob. He was cold, he was scared, and he was alone. He wondered if the police had arrested Red. He was afraid he never again would see his old friend.

When Bob woke up the next morning, he started sneezing and coughing. He was so cold, he couldn't stop shivering. He needed to get warm, but he didn't dare turn on his motor. Someone might hear him and call the police.

Then he heard a sound coming from the highway. It wasn't the police car or any other car. And it wasn't a truck. It was a tractor, and it sounded like Red!

When Bob heard Red's tires roll onto the bridge, he called out, "Hey, Red! Stop!"

Red stopped quickly and called down, "Is that you, Bob?"

"Yes! It's me!" Bob yelled. "I'm under the bridge!"

"Are you okay?" asked Red.

"I'm all wet and I'm awfully cold," Bob told him, "and I was shot in my left-rear fender."

"I know," said Red, "but can you make it up the slope?"

"I think I can," replied Bob.

After he had sneezed and coughed several more times, Bob's motor sputtered to a start. Then he drove slowly up the slope to the highway.

"The police caught the robbers," Red told him, "so they aren't after us anymore."

"I'm glad to hear that," replied Bob. Then he noticed that Red's seat was empty. "Where's the scarecrow?" he asked.

"He fell off during the chase," explained Red.

"Well," said Bob thoughtfully, "maybe no one will notice that you don't have a driver."

"I hope not," Red agreed. "But we had better get going before there's more traffic. We're only an hour away from Birchville."

"Okay," groaned Bob. "I'll try to make it."

The old truck sputtered again, then finally began to move forward.

With Red in the lead, they pulled onto the highway. Once again, they were on their way to the antique automotive museum — their last hope for survival.

When the sun began to come up, Red called back, "Hurry up, Bob."

Bob tried to go as fast as Red, but he couldn't. Red noticed that his friend was lagging behind. He stopped several times and waited for Bob to catch up.

The old truck shook and rattled, and it coughed and sputtered. Trying with all his might to keep going, Bob leaned forward and strained every cylinder he had. But he felt so cold, and he was so exhausted. When he came to a long hill, he had to pull over to the side of the highway and stop.

When Red saw Bob wasn't moving, he quickly turned around and hurried back to his friend.

"What's the matter?" he asked.

"It's the end of the road for me," Bob answered. "My distributor is rusty, and my points are all worn down. I can't make it up this hill."

"But we can't stop now," Red urged. "We've got just a few more miles to go."

"I know," said Bob, "but I don't think I can make it."

"You've got to!" Red insisted.

"I can't," Bob replied, gasping for breath. "I want you to go on without me. At least one of us can make it to the museum."

"I can't go on without you," Red told him. "You're the best friend I've ever had."

"You have to save yourself," said Bob.

"No!" Red replied firmly. "I won't leave you!"

Red gunned his motor. Then he turned around and backed up. He hooked his tow chain around Bob's front bumper.

"Hang on, old Buddy!" he called to Bob. "You and I are going to Birchville *together!*"

"I'm too heavy for you to pull," Bob tried to tell him.

But Red wouldn't listen. He revved up his motor instead. Then he leaned forward. He pulled and he groaned. The chain grew tight as Red strained and towed his friend up the hill.

Bob and Red finally reached the town of Birchville. There were more cars on the road now. But no one seemed to notice that the old tractor didn't have a driver.

Then Bob and Red saw the sign they were looking for —
THE ANTIQUE AUTOMOTIVE MUSEUM — Turn Right.

They turned right, then Red pulled Bob through the gate and up the driveway. They stopped in front of the main building.

"When the owner gets here," said Red, "we'll find out if he wants an old truck and an old tractor."

They did not have very long to wait. In a few minutes, a big 1948 Cadillac, all shined and polished, pulled into the driveway. It stopped next to Bob and Red, and a man opened the door and got out.

"Say, where did the two of you come from?" the man asked.

Bob and Red held their breaths. They were afraid the man wouldn't want them and would turn them away. Instead, the man opened the door of the old blue truck and looked inside. Then he walked over to

the tractor and gave Red a friendly pat.

"I'm glad you're here," the man said with a smile. "You old fellas are real beauties. We're going to overhaul your motors and smooth out your dents. And we'll give you a couple of coats of paint and shine up your bumpers. When you're all fixed up, we'll put you in the museum for everyone to admire.

True to his word, that's exactly what the man did.

After Bob and Red were completely restored, they glistened like new. Both of them stood in the museum, side by side, as best friends like to do.

People came from miles around to see Bob and Red. They enjoyed looking at the two old-timers.

"If only they could talk," one visitor said, "I'll bet this truck and tractor would have some interesting stories to tell."

Bob the Truck and Red the Tractor didn't say a word. They just looked at each other and smiled.

BOOKS FOR STUDENTS BY STUDENTS

Dav Pilkey
age 19

Lauren Peters
age 7

Benjamin Kendall
age 7

Amy Hagstrom
age 9

Michael Cain
age 11

Leslie A. MacKeen
age 9

Shintaro Maeda
age 8

A. Chandrasekhar
age 9

Dennis Vollmer
age 6

Alise Leggat
age 8

Walking is Wild Weird and Wacky
written and illustrated by
Karen Kerber
by Karen Kerber, age 12
St. Louis, Missouri
ISBN 0-933849-29-X   Full Color

THE DRAGON OF ORD
written and illustrated by
DAVID McADOO
by David McAdoo, age 14
Springfield, Missouri
ISBN 0-933849-23-0   Inside Duotone

Strong and Free
written and illustrated by
Amy Hagstrom
by Amy Hagstrom, age 9
Portola, California
ISBN 0-933849-15-X   Full Color

ME AND MY VEGGIES
WRITTEN AND ILLUSTRATED BY
ISAAC WHITLATCH
by Isaac Whitlatch, age 11
Casper, Wyoming
ISBN 0-933849-16-8   Full Color

WHO CAN FIX IT?
written & illustrated by
Leslie Ann MacKeen
by Leslie Ann MacKeen, age 9
Winston-Salem, North Carolina
ISBN 0-933849-19-2   Full Color

ELMER the GRUMP
- written & illustrated by -
ELIZABETH HAIDLE
by Elizabeth Haidle, age 13
Beaverton, Oregon
ISBN 0-933849-20-6   Full Color

Taddy McFinley and the Great Grey Grimly
written & illustrated by
Heidi Salter
by Heidi Salter, age 19
Berkeley, California
ISBN 0-933849-21-4   Full Color

Problems at the North Pole
written & illustrated by
Lauren Peters
by Lauren Peters, age 7
Kansas City, Missouri
ISBN 0-933849-25-7   Full Color

OLIVER and the OIL SPILL
written and illustrated by
ARUNA CHANDRASEKHAR
by Aruna Chandrasekhar, age 9
Houston, Texas
ISBN 0-933849-33-8   Full Color

Life in the ghetto
written and illustrated by
ANIKA D. THOMAS
by Anika Thomas, age 13
Pittsburgh, Pennsylvania
ISBN 0-933849-34-6   Inside Two Colors

A STONE PROMISE
BY CARA REICHEL
by Cara Reichel, age 15
Rome, Georgia
ISBN 0-933849-35-4   Inside Two Colors

PATULOU, THE PRAIRIE RATTLESNAKE
written and illustrated by
JONATHAN KAHN
by Jonathan Kahn, age 9
Richmond Heights, Ohio
ISBN 0-933849-36-2   Full Color

ALIEN INVASIONS
written and illustrated by
BENJAMIN KENDALL
by Benjamin Kendall, age 7
State College, Pennsylvania
ISBN 0-933849-42-7   Full Color

FOGBOUND
written and illustrated by
STEVEN SHEPARD
by Steven Shepard, age 13
Great Falls, Virginia
ISBN 0-933849-43-5   Full Color

CHANGES
written and illustrated by
TRAVIS WILLIAMS
by Travis Williams, age 16
Sardis, B.C., Canada
ISBN 0-933849-44-3   Inside Two Colors

A SPECIAL DAY
written & illustrated by
DUBRAVKA KOLANOVIĆ
by Dubravka Kolanović, age
Savannah, Georgia
ISBN 0-933849-45-1   Full Color

THE NATIONAL WRITTEN & ILLUSTRATED BY...AWARD WINNERS

WORLD WAR WON
by Dav Pilkey, age 19
Cleveland, Ohio
ISBN 0-933849-22-2   Full Color

JOSHUA DISOBEYS
by Dennis Vollmer, age 6
Grove, Oklahoma
ISBN 0-933849-12-5   Full Color

THE HALF & HALF DOG
by Lisa Gross, age 12
Santa Fe, New Mexico
ISBN 0-933849-13-3   Full Color

WHO OWNS THE SUN?
by Stacy Chbosky, age 14
Pittsburgh, Pennsylvania
ISBN 0-933849-14-1   Full Color

the Legend of SIR MIGUEL
by Michael Cain, age 11
Annapolis, Maryland
ISBN 0-933849-26-5   Full Color

WE ARE A THUNDERSTORM
by Amity Gaige, age 16
Reading, Pennsylvania
ISBN 0-933849-27-3   Full Color

BROKEN ARROW BOY
by Adam Moore, age 9
Broken Arrow, Oklahoma
ISBN 0-933849-24-9   Inside Duotone

GET THAT GOAT!
by Michael Aushenker, age 19
Ithaca, New York
ISBN 0-933849-28-1   Full Color

TOO MUCH TRICK OR TREAT
by Jayna Miller, age 19
Zanesville, Ohio
ISBN 0-933849-37-0   Full Color

PUNT, PASS & POINT!
by Bonnie-Alise Leggat, age 8
Culpepper, Virginia
ISBN 0-933849-39-7   Full Color

NINA'S MAGIC
by Lisa Kirsten Butenhoff, age 13
Woodbury, Minnesota
ISBN 0-933849-40-0   Full Color

JAMBI AND THE LIONS
by Jennifer Brady, age 17
Columbia, Missouri
ISBN 0-933849-41-9   Full Color

Abracadabra
by Amy Jones, age 17
Shirley, Arkansas
ISBN 0-933849-46-X   Full Color

THOMAS RACCOON'S FANTASTIC AIRSHOW
by Shintaro Maeda, age 8
Wichita, Kansas
ISBN 0-933849-51-6   Full Color

THE SUNFLOWER
by Miles MacGregor, age 12
Phoenix, Arizona
ISBN 0-933849-52-4   Full Color

THE SHADOW SHOP
by Kristin Pedersen, age 18
Etobicoke, Ont., Canada
ISBN 0-933849-53-2   Full Color

Travis Williams
age 16

Anika D. Thomas
age 13

Isaac Whitlatch
age 11

Elizabeth Haidle
age 13

Miles MacGregor
age 12

Jayna Miller
age 19

Jonathan Kahn
age 9

Stacy Chbosky
age 14

David McAdoo
age 12

Amity Gaige
age 16